D0398390

The Tiny Book of Tiny Stories

volume ① 2 3

!t books • an imprint of harpercollinspublishers

Printed in China

HarperCollins books may be purchased for educational, business, or
sales promotional use. For information please write: Special Markets
Department, HarperCollins Publishers, 10 East 53rd Street,
New York, NY 10022.

FIRST EDITION

ISBN 978-0-06-212166-0

13 14 15 SCP 10 9 8 7

"The universe is not made of atoms;
it's made of $\overset{tiny}{\underset{\wedge}{}}$ stories."

-Muriel Rukeyser & wirrow

Another Introductory Interview

Are we recording? Regular JOE here!
Joining me in the REC Room again is
the original Tiny Story teller himself, the
ever effusive and always anonymous wirrow!

[○REC]

hi joe.

So wirrow, the "Tiny Stories"
collaboration you started back
in the spring of 2010 has now
blossomed into a veritable
phenomenon, with countless
contributions pouring in from all
over the world! In fact, even as
I speak, and as our dear readers
read, hit RECord's creative
collective has already begun work
on next year's volume.
Any words of encouragement to
all those writers and illustrators
reading this who can visit:
HITRECORD.ORG/TinyStories2
to get involved?

wirrow...?

Any words of encouragement...?

hit
record

..oh! er yeah,
get involved guys.

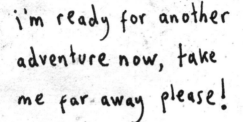

Ok one more...
but then YOU have
to read to ME!

The Sun is such a lonely star.

Whenever he comes out to see
his friends, they all disappear.

As the sugar cube sank in the cup of tea, he did his best Wicked Witch of the West.

"I'm melting," he screamed, "MELTING!"

The motes of dust in the
window's light danced
with such delish delight
that she joined them.

King Midas often
wondered what would happen
if he touched himself.

"Okay, I'll admit, I have a few skeletons in my closet; but they weren't skeletons when I put them there."

You're gone. No mailing address.

But I send you letters anyway.

I don't get dressed anymore.

I just don't feel like it.

The doctor's wife ate two
apples a day, just to be safe.

But her husband kept
coming home.

just before i died, my life
flashed before my eyes.

but it flashed so slowly
that i lived it all again.

and again and again...

There are times

when girls kiss just for fun.

"I didn't disappear.

Everything else did!"

DODOS DID-DID BUT T

X-rays made her feel like a model,
the doctors taking her pictures.

She always posed.

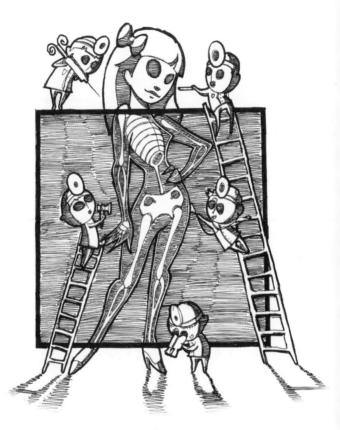

I collect flickering stars

in old pickling jars,

poking holes in the lids

so they can breathe.

The mumble bee had a fuzzy buzz.

When he tried to say "honey,"
it came out all funny...

One day before breakfast, an
orange rolled off the counter
and escaped its fate, bounding
happily through the kitchen door.

Filled with hope,
the egg followed.

The element of surprise wasn't
allowed near the Periodic Table.

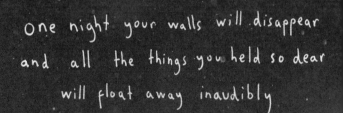

One night your walls will disappear
and all the things you held so dear
will float away inaudibly .

"It's HE-RO," the boy argued.

"No," the girl insisted,
"it's HER-O."

The outsider stood beside

The little low tide, as it dried

And he sighed as he decided,

"We'd be better off inside."

Sometimes, I lie awake wondering
about the future, when I lie
awake wondering about the past.

The hostess offered seconds,
but the guests were stuffed.

In winter, when the leaves
have gone, the owls swoop in
to keep the trees warm.

OH... is it like a "dress smart" kinda place? :)

I fear I might be paranoid.

please

repeat

your

proposition

ONE WANTED TO SHARE A LIFE TOGETHER

THE OTHER WANTED TO SHARE TWO

In the end, he just
decided to call it an early
Christmas decoration.

SIMPLE

Is it going to hurt?

no.
It's going to be simple and painless.

you can't sleep?

me either.

let's can't sleep together.

I know other worlds exist.

I can see them
in my peripheral vision.

THE TINIEST STORY

Once upon a time, there was

The End.

A man touched me:
his hand... my thigh.

I touched him too:
my fist... his jaw.

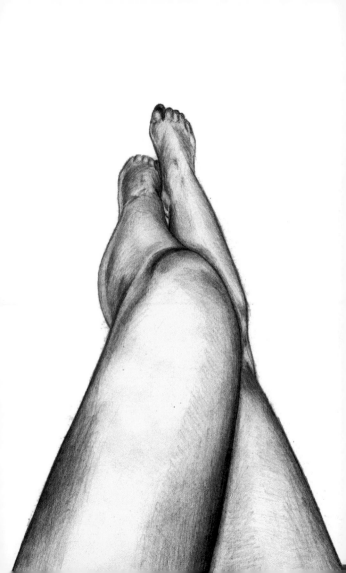

His hands were weak and shaking
from carrying far too many
books from the bookshop.

It was the best feeling.

When people have insomnia, they lie awake all night watching TV.

When raccoons have insomnia, they go catch a matinee.

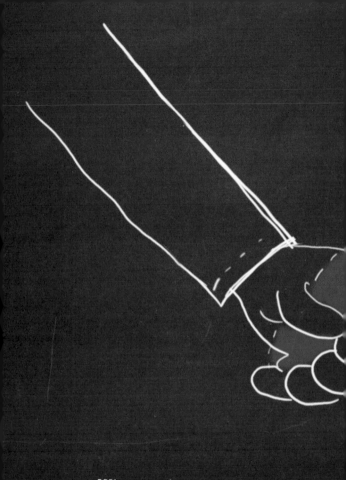

When you become a ghost

feel free to haunt me.

The shots rang out again
today, and I was sad to see
the gallant gator go.

But I couldn't help a sorry smile
knowing the dry guys would have
no appetite left for turtle soup.

One night Death came to visit me

And offered me a cup of tea.

I did not mention it was cold

And carefully sipped around the mold.

"Well, look who I ran into,"
crowed Coincidence.

"Please," flirted Fate, "this
was meant to be."

If I read our story backwards,
it's about how I un-broke
your heart, and then we were
happy until one day, you
forgot about me forever.

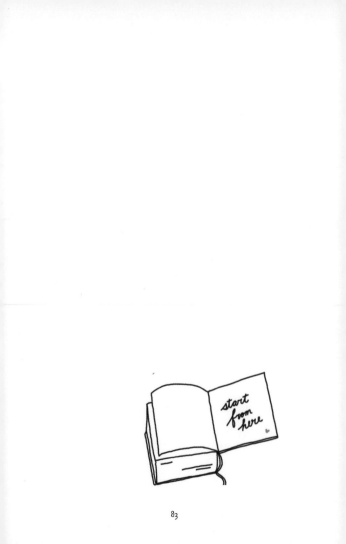

start
from
here

RESOURCES:

p.	contributor	record no.
		www.hitrecord.org/records/record no.
cover	wirrow	491124
04-05	RegularJOE, wirrow	
06-07	wirrow	447439
08	KarizzMarie	313548
09	wen, wirrow,	448384, 366710
	Lea Daniel, lokiii	412589, 438598
10	lindzey42, RegularJOE	69245, 456836
11	JacksonBlack	448602
12	janetfelts,	417804,
	arafel3873, cacheth	410965, 417681
13	wirrow, RegularJOE	68799, 442837
14	smweed	415680
15	Susano987	417649
16-17	Eskapurla, MadisenMusic	447632, 427841
18	RegularJOE, Dina	457410, 440614
19	mirtle	429253
20	MattConley	416656
21	InkedCanvas	445976
22	bryn-haz	123588
23	MelonBerri	450108
24	rowrowrow	407991
25	wen	447236
26	likeadisco, RedheadViv	451313, 453539
27	wirrow, Metaphorest	453667, 345219
28-29	Metaphorest	421954
30	alpal	274887
31	Anatole baptiste	438918

p.	contributor	record no.

www.hitrecord.org/records/record no.

p.	contributor	record no.
32	thedustdancestoo	438268
33	tori, Marke	89913, 497553
34	Metaphorest	418183
35	Rimfrost	447681
36	Sparksee05	220621
37	cat-cat	452393
38	bryn-haz, RegularJOE	417057, 419667
	rejjie	421708
39	wirrow	474083
40	InkedCanvas	411917
41	Unusual Suspect	416247
42	Michal	435444
43	Eskapurla, Readmooses	441118, 440477
44	brokenRECords, RegularJOE	435701, 439010
45	Rimfrost	437720
46-47	mirtle, InkedCanvas, RegularJOE	436925, 436538, 457287
48	Metaphorest	439847
49	elayne	439718
50-51	wirrow	377156
52	MaxBrixton	432444
53	JacksonBlack	442507
54-55	wirrow	456684
56	RegularJOE	446038
	totallyjamie, yes-you-am	446242, 458546
57	yes-you-am	441829

p.	contributor	record no.

58–59	wirrow	69059
60	thedustdancestoo	439207
61	chelsea.e	458030
62	Readmooses	431482
63	phenomenaaa, RegularJOE	429833, 457002
64–65	Haus-of-Glitch, Eskapurla	215079, 434647
66	InkedCanvas	349243
67	Dolphin170, featherpetal	242474, 443223
68	sallyeloo	266857
69	Consh	276464
70	MadisenMusic, RegularJOE	416748, 421128
	Susano987	419181
71	Day Glo, RegularJOE	423981, 439176
	paperlilies	459169
72–73	thedustdancestoo, Nevertime	438800, 444775
74	RegularJOE	458542
75	chelsea.e	455773
76–77	catsolen	29128
78	DianeFT	451607
79	crayfish	451512
80	left-coast-jane, Reverie	449780, 448087
81	Maliboo	451930
82	Blodnasir	438344
83	heidi101	440640
ends	totallyjamie	455594

with additional illustrations by: ashleyrosed, Syoh, wirrow, Attilee, Greatflydini, Unusual Suspect, RedHeadMonster, Rimfrost, reijie, Metaphorest, Susano987, arafel3873, mcjammycustard, mirtle, slvitale, JacksonBlack, & MelonBerri

ABOUT HITRECORD

hitRECord is the open-collaborative production company founded and directed by actor and artist Joseph Gordon-Levitt. We create and develop art and media collectively using our website where anyone with an internet connection can upload his or her records, download and remix others' records, and work on projects together. When the results of our work and play are produced and make money, hitRECord splits the profits 50/50 with everybody who contributed to the final production.

Thanks again <3

THE TINY BOOK OF TINY STORIES
volume 1

Directed by Joseph Gordon-Levitt
Produced by Jared Geller
Creative Direction, Layout & Design by Marke Johnson
Original Concept & Creative Direction by wirrow